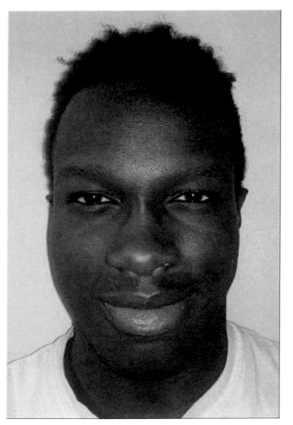

Author's Note:

Hello my name is Mark Ladu. I'm a creative writing student at Washington high school, whose interests involves art, literature, explorations, adventure, and geography.

This book is dedicated to Mrs. Halgerson, Mrs. Smith, Mrs. Blair, and lastly to Mrs. Kolbeck.

Ty was their guardian. He brought them to work and introduced them to everyone, including his boss.

2

First came Ari, the leader of the group, and next came his lovely twin sister Lisa.

3

Then there came Berry, the genius of the four, and last, but not least, came Jambo, who was very strong and loved bananas.

4

Throughout the day, things were pretty normal until the emergency alarm went off, "Houston we have a problem."

"Someone, anyone, please save my husband," said Mrs. Clark.

7

9

"Here, take these suits, you'll need them for your mission," said Chief.

The team suited up in the colorful space suits.

5, 4, 3, 2, 1

12

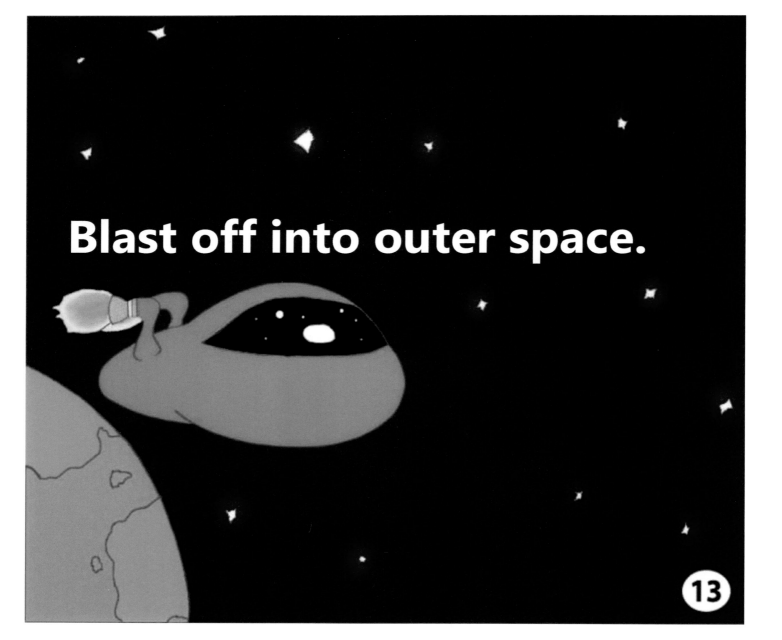

Blast off into outer space.

13

On the way, everyone had their own role: Ari was the captain, Berry was the pilot, Lisa was the doctor and, well, for Jambo, he had eaten all the bananas he could find.

14

But suddenly, they came across a big purple planet. "Brace yourselves, we're here. Welcome to Andromeda," Berry said.

16

They rushed toward the sound and found that Jumbo tried to eat Commander Clark.

"Jambo, spit him out right now!" yelled Lisa.

21

When they got home, everyone at NASA was proud for what the crew had done. The Chief congratulated them for their heroic deed.

26

Ty was very proud of what they did, so proud he wanted to give them a name, a name they could go by.

The End

43633736R00021

Made in the USA
Middletown, DE
14 May 2017